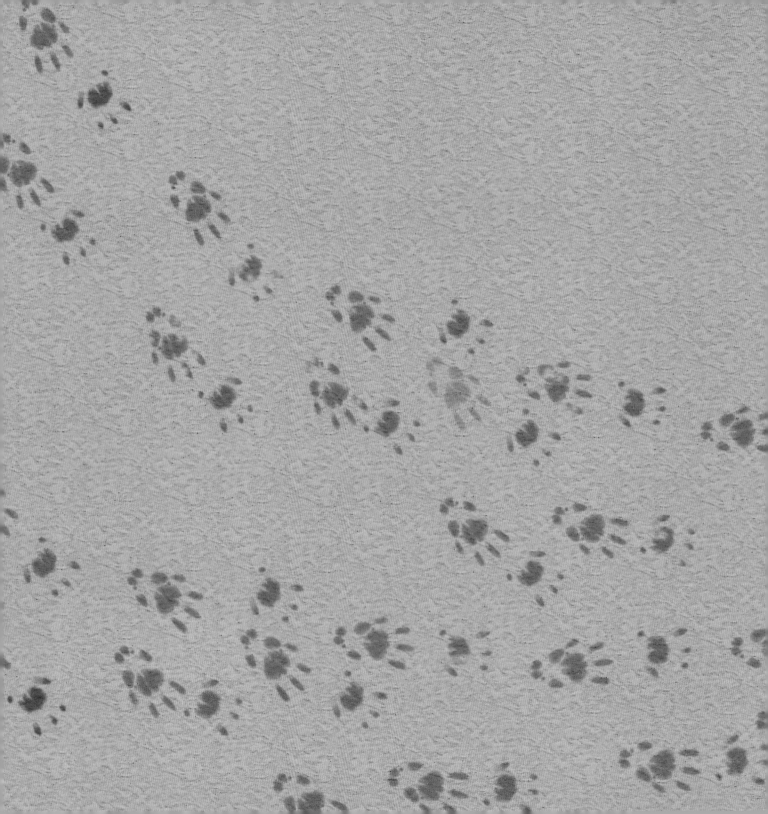

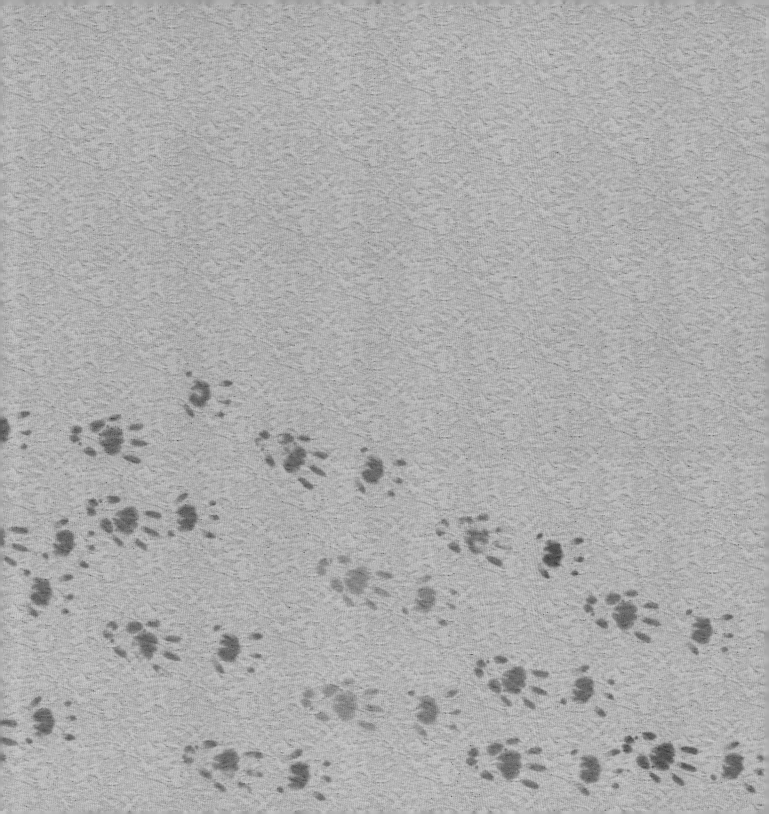

The Heavenly Hedgehog

Mili
Joni

3 norai

On a clear night, in a wood lit by the moon,
to the sound of a nightingale singing,
three hoglets were born to two happy hedgehogs.

They were born blind,
covered with soft,
light quills.

In two weeks, the little hedgehogs will gain their sight, and when they grow up, they will have as many as 5000 quills!

The parents named the liveliest and most curious hoglet Quilly.

"Butterflies love to play tag and... tickle your nose!"

"Oh! Mmm..."

His sister Needles and his brother Prickles quickly caught up with him.

"Strawberries are fragrant and juicy!"

Once the hoglets were a little older, their parents decided
to visit a distant relative of theirs – a porcupine
who lived in Brazil.

But the hoglets were still too small to go along with them. The journey would have been too long, too far, and too difficult. So the hoglets stayed with their Grandpa Sage.

Grandpa had loads to do, all day long...

Help Grandpa find:

- his compass

- his binoculars

- his alarm clock

- his drawing compass

- his telescope

But the hoglets were anything but bored.

"Swimming is fun! The water is refreshing!"

There was a family of beavers living in a nearby dam.
The sharp-toothed neighbours taught the hoglets how to swim.

Together, the friends played
catch and hide-and-seek;

they rolled logs
and fished to
their heart's
content.

"A beaver's teeth never stop growing!"

When the first stars began to shine,
Grandpa Sage would grab
his magical device – his telescope – and climb up
with his grandchildren closer to the heavens.

"When you see a shooting star, make a wish and it'll come true!"

The telescope
brought the sky, the shining stars,
and the distant planets closer than ever.

Mercury

Mars

The Sun

Jupiter

Venus

Saturn

Neptune

Pluto

Uranus

The Moon

The time they spent with Grandpa was simply MAGICAL!

Earth

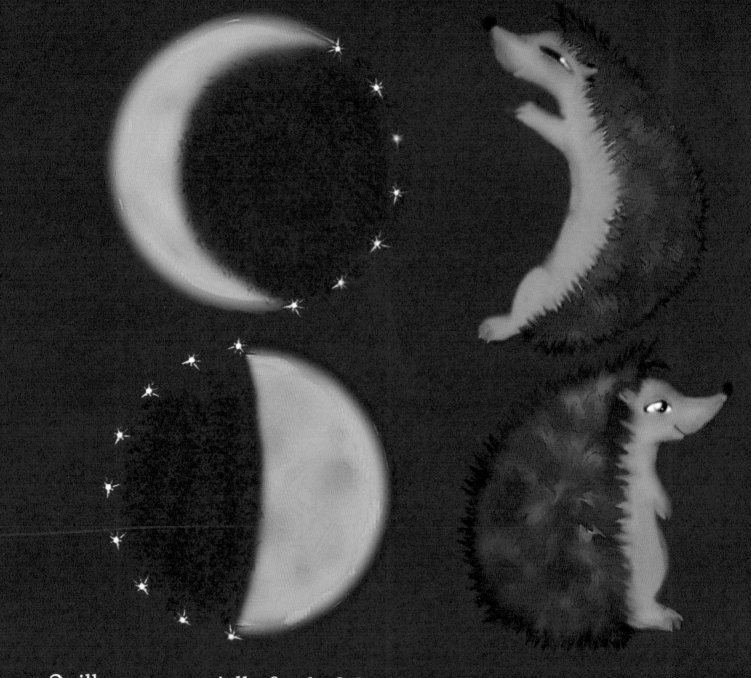

Quilly was especially fond of the glowing Moon, which was constantly changing. The Moon reminded the hoglet of himself...

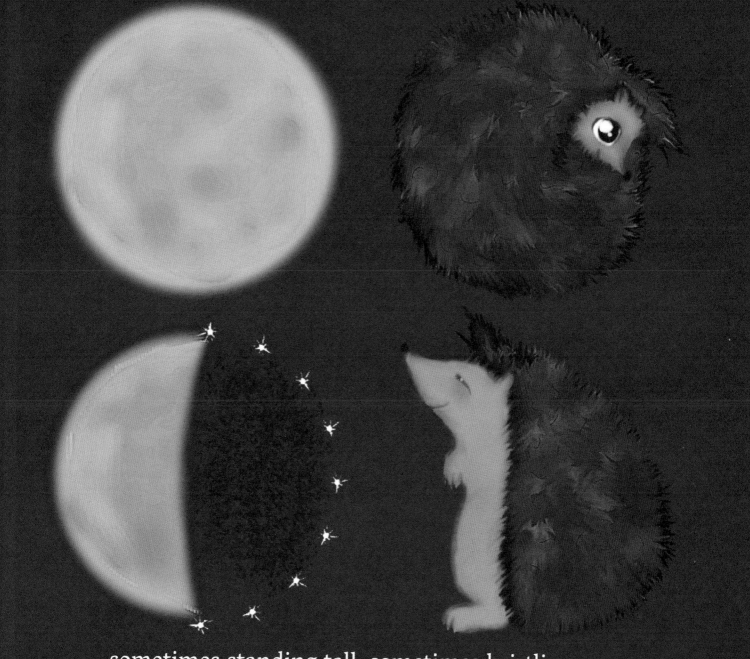

...sometimes standing tall, sometimes bristling,
and sometimes rolled into a tight ball.

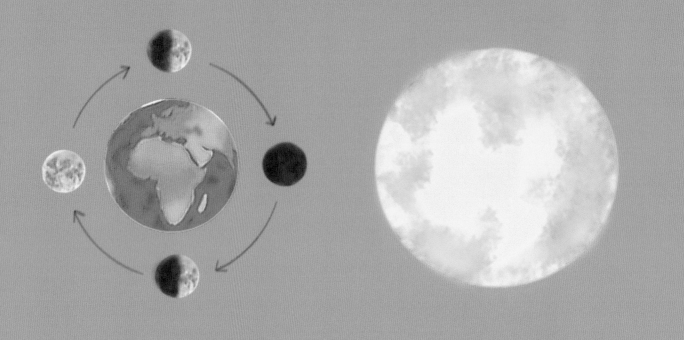

Grandpa explained that
the Moon doesn't actually glow.
It orbits our planet – Earth –
and reflects the light of the Sun.

We only see the part of the Moon
that is lit up, which is why
it seems to change shape.

Those shapes are known as the phases of the Moon.

There are four of them: - new moon

 - first quarter

 - full moon

 - last quarter

What a mysterious heavenly body!
In fact, it's always rolled into a ball!

To himself, the hoglet called the Moon...

...the
Heavenly
Hedgehog.

Grandpa also said that the Moon is almost 400,000 kilometres away.

That's 80 times more than a hedgehog has quills!

If hedgehogs drove cars, they could travel to the Moon and back in two years.

In autumn, their mum and dad
came back from their trip.
They brought the hoglets greetings
and souvenirs from Brazil.

They also brought them
a fantastic gift – a football ball
that looked just like the full Moon.

The spiny mammals spent the last warm days of the year
with their beaver friends, playing with the ball
in a forest clearing.

The days grew shorter,
the temperatures
began to drop,
and it rained
more and more.

The hedgehog family got ready to hibernate.
Under an old, rooty tree stump, they built a cosy,
warm nest from grass and leaves.
And that is where they will sleep, until spring,
when the first swallows return.

As his eyes began to close,
Quilly dreamed of meeting the Heavenly Hedgehog.

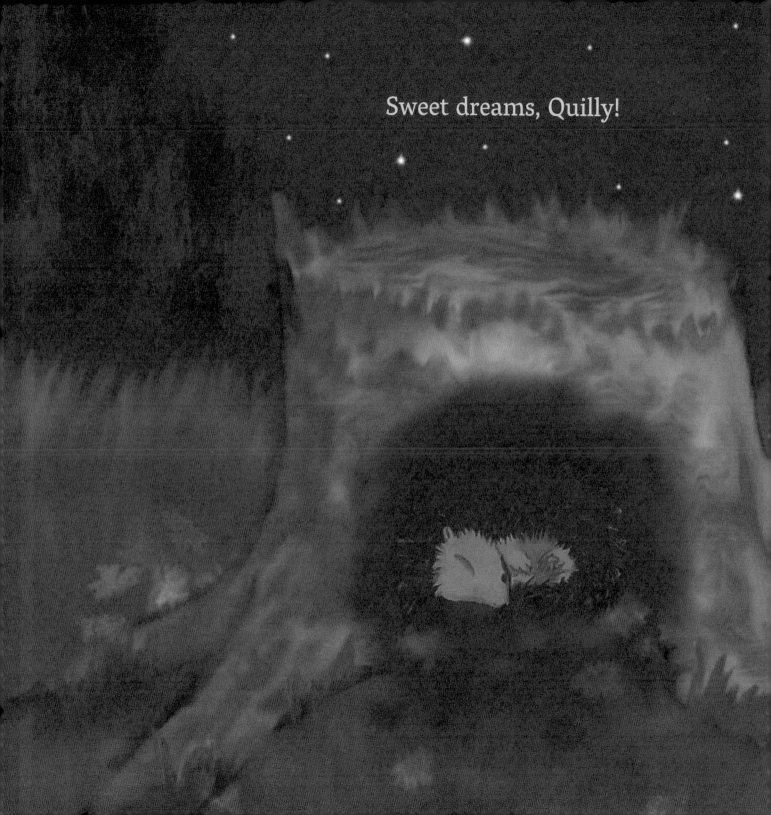

Sweet dreams, Quilly!

The Heavenly Hedgehog

Vilnius, 2020

ISBN 978-609-96161-2-4 (e-book)

ISBN 978-609-96161-3-1 (printed book)

The book can be purchased at https://www.3norai.lt/books/the-heavenly-hedgehog

Printed in Great Britain
by Amazon